SALUTE

SALUTE

*A
Novella*

MAYA BECHI

Robson and Puritan

CONTENTS

To my father the Army man. The Griot.
&
To Buihe "Skillz" Madu who makes expression possible and abundant.

Salute: A Novella
By Maya Hicks Bechi

DEDICATION

To my father the army man. The griot.

&

To Buihe "Skillz" Madu who makes expression possible and abundant.

This page left blank intentionally

Oblivious

"Bleed! Bleed! Bleed!"

The staff sergeant was crouched low in the corner like a wounded animal as those three words growled from his mouth. At the shouting, the military policemen turned around to face the newly detained soldier. The corporal on duty, also hearing the commotion, ran from his office to see what in the hell could have happened in a matter of seconds since they left his sight.

"Bleed! Bleed! Bleed!" the staff sergeant continued to cry out as he mercilessly slashed at his own wrists with the blade he'd found in his nearby toiletry kit. Blood rained down on the patches and his uniform which lay in a heap on the floor. Upon arrest he had been instructed to remove the rank insignia from his clothing. That command had ripped his soul apart. As each string of thread loosened, he recounted the hours of drills, the physical training, the mental dedication. and the late nights studying and perfecting every directive and segment of the U.S. Army standard operating procedures. His mind raced through the years he'd spent training to be prepared, as if by instinct, for the time when he would be in enemy territory defending freedom. With rapid succession he calculated the number of men who had been trained under him, and those among them intrinsically motivated to become the best. The Korean War had ended, and this was supposed to be a time of peace and preparation, a time to defend this country against any impending foreign threats. Yet, these had been the most challenging times in his personal history with the American Army.

How did he arrive to this moment and not remember why? The dishonor of losing his rank and removing the symbols that acknowledged his commitment was a deplorable feeling. For now, it was better to use the blade on himself and thereby restoring honor and valor in the way he had learned Japanese Samurai did in the history books. With each touch and plunge of the sharp edge to his exposed skin, a sense of relief washed over him. This act would achieve greater admiration than the former. He closed his eyes and drank deep from the imagined vision of his mother, his father, and his own sense of pride regarding this decision. The decision to end it all. Death. It would be better than to continue the ceremony of removing the proofs of all he had worked for with his soul and strength, and ironically, his blood. His eyes began to burn as he looked at the insignia on the floor at his knees and his khaki standard issue uniform to his right. His unit had been one of the first to completely convert all soldiers to the new uniform standards. Another accomplishment he had achieved among these men while leading them. As a black man, it was no small feat to win over the trust and commitment of his unit. Sure, they were taught to obey higher ranking soldiers because of the safety it provides when in hostile territory, but it is much different in reality to have the voluntary commitment of trust.

He looked again at the green and gold staff sergeant patch. Without that patch, there was no way to tell the difference from an enlisted or an officer. He felt the rush of bile reaching his throat as he considered the ranks of the men surrounding him now. All white, and all lower ranking than himself. The very men he commanded day to day. Now, they were in charge and demanding that he remove his victories. Piece by piece.

The military police surrounded him, lifting him from the floor and restraining him against the wall in order to pry the razor blade from his fingers. Each of them stood about six feet tall while trying to gain control inside of a six by eight space. The floors had become slippery and had it not been for their updated, full rubber sole M1948 boots, they would have had to manage it all jiu-jitsu style.

"Sergeant Anthony! Sir! Sir! Sir!" they took turns shouting. The room began to fill with the thick smell of struggle. The humidity caused by the sweat of the men mixed with the metallic scent of Lawrence Anthony's blood surrounded them like a heavy duvet.

"What in the hell just happened?!" demanded Corporal Monty

"He just went crazy, sir! We don't know why! We need a medic!"

Lawrence seemed disconnected from the rest of the room, his strength was super human adrenaline assisted and he was determined to die in that moment so he lifted one MP and tossed him aside like a ragdoll. As two more rushed in to subdue him, Lawrence had enough time to land a solid punch on the other, grab the razor blade once again, and start in on the second wrist. By this time there were no more tears threatening to fill his eyes, just a steely cold determination to make good with his internal promise to end this suffering once and for good. This was only his fifth year in the Army. He was inflamed with patriotism, had plans to retire from here after fulfilling a dream and living out what he thought was his purpose. While the majority of the branch's enlisted were obtained because of the draft, Lawrence had been of the minority who had volunteered to enlist. There was so much he had disregarded as inferior when compared to this calling of serving his country. "Land of the free, home of the brave." To say that he was proud would be a severe misrepresentation and an understatement of the true level of commitment and pride he embodied. After several more minutes of struggle, Staff Sergeant Lawrence Anthony crumpled to the cold hard concrete and drifted into sweet oblivion.

***

Birth and Good Home Training

The dining room table was mahogany, embellished with touches of mother of pearl along the concave portions of the luxurious side carvings. It was exquisite. Many gatherings had taken place there, but none as eventful as the one taking place this morning. The length of the table stretched down the center of the dining room, firmly anchored in place by its heftiness. Flanking the table stood a patient, a doctor, and trepidatious set of parents. Mr. and Mrs. Belle, with great care, had made a space for their daughter in the middle of the dining room when birthing pains had increased beyond her ability to bear.

The child was born at 8:45 a.m. among the vaulted ceilings, sweeping drapes, and watchful eyes. Dr. Myers delivered a healthy baby boy with the assistance of a midwife. This was Dr. Myers' first home delivery as an obstetrician and luckily the midwife was none other than Mrs. Belle herself. She and her husband were the parents of the sixteen-year-old girl who was giving birth to their first grandchild on their brand-new Jacobean dining table. Evelyn, although only sixteen, was a new wife and already fully entrenched in her journey into motherhood. Their marriage was every bit a shotgun wedding. Her husband, Richard, was still young himself. Only eighteen-years-old.

Mr. and Mrs. Belle had consistently guided Evelyn with a strong hand all her life. She was an Elder's daughter and was required to exemplify full respect and cooperation in all matters for the sake of his eldership title. It was biblical. Not only was it important for her to be raised and grounded in spiritual matters, but she was their eldest child and would have all rights to the legacy, foundation, and execution of the family estate. Her reputation in the community would be the direct and sole reflection of the family name.

Mr. and Mrs. Belle had met as undergrads at Fisk University, travelled together up north after graduation during the great migration to Chicago, and there established their roots as activists, clergy, and sole owners of a modest insurance agency. Mr. Belle's induction into the brotherhood of Sigma Pi Phi was seamless and occurred at a well-appointed time. The brotherhood was infamously known as the Boulé, or, Council of Chiefs. Being counted among the Boulé meant that you became a source of community support for those on their pathway to financial, career, and leadership opportunities. Every member was committed to using their status and successful climb out of underserved communities to elevate and enhance those of same communities. The Belles were at the forefront of the struggle for equality in the south and west sides of Chicago. Young men and women were hosted in their homes regularly as Mrs. Belle's decision to work from home afforded them the privilege of stoking, sponsoring, and championing the ambitious desires of the collective community. They were the clan to learn from if you wanted to become more prosperous and self-sufficient.

Mrs. Belle came from a long line of freedmen and was not the first among her kinfolk to attend a University, nor was she unaccustomed to the freedoms that financial liberation provided. During the bank run of the Depression era, her father was known for how he "had the resolve and faith like Abraham" to let his deposits lay just as they were and not snatch them out of their respective investments. As God would have it, they barely held on through the turmoil of the Depression, but held on they did. As a result, Mrs. Belle's trust fund became the breath of life to the Belles' dreams of becoming self-supporting clergy.

"No one will ever say we took the church's money," she would say. Consistently frugal, always poised and polished without a hair out of place, and elegantly dressed to fit every curve of her size six frame, Belle was a belle. She was a classic beauty with a well-proportioned face and delicate features and although a socialite, she took pride in keeping things simple.

She and Mr. Belle were a perfect complement for each other and reared Evelyn with consistent intent toward understanding her privilege and her plight as an American who is classified as black. Ultimately, their decision to move from Chicago to Detroit before Evelyn gave birth had everything to do with ensuring Evelyn, Richard, and the baby had the best chance of establishing a solid foundation for themselves. Mr. Belle immediately called on every connection and resource he had within The Grand Boulé, resolved not to allow his pride to become an obstacle when vying for support for his new son-in-law Richard. As one of the newer members of Sigma Pi Phi, Mr. Belle learned very quickly why they adapted the name Boulé. This fraternity of brothers were truly noblemen in their own rights. They were indeed committed to serving the community, had strong bonds of brotherhood, focused on bridging economic gaps, and strove for excellence in all things while never forgetting spirituality. Every man blazoned with the name Grand Boulé understood that their successes in business and elevation to the economically upper class was not the result of their good grades, abilities and talents, or the schools they attended, no, it was also a result of having received some help along the way.

At the heart of the Belles' home, bursting from the warm, cinnamon, and nutmeg scented kitchen, came a constant efflux of robust energy of youth, politics, and determination permeating the house and the grounds it stood upon. Among them, their new son-in-law, Richard Anthony, shined like Moose Peak Lighthouse through a foggy day in Maine. He stood five feet, five inches tall, with a high yellow skin tone and deep brown eyes that locked you in with his geniality. He had the stature and physique of a manual laborer and a heart as pure as gold. Like most families living in the south and west sides during that time, Richard's family had migrated when their farm failed. It was easy to love Richard, even though this was a hard time for light skinned blacks among their own people. Colorism ran long and cut deep hurtful ravines through generations of some families. Yet, Richard had a way of intertwining himself among people of all backgrounds and economic statuses, like a chameleon blending in. There likely wasn't a soul in all of Chicago who didn't like him.

The Belles had known about Richard and Evelyn's romantic affinity and desire to marry, however, they didn't know about the urgent need nestled and growing inside her tiny womb. It was seen as God's grace to the family name that her parents had said yes to the marriage just months before and they could respectably deliver their first grandchild and announce it to the congregation.

Finally, the day arrived when her labor pains began. The vitality of youth and the benefits of her age carried her through the twenty-eight-hour labor. Evelyn was visibly tired, but not exhausted. When you studied her face a little deeper, what you recognized was the surprise, joy, and relief of having made it through to the other side of the birthing journey.

"What time is it?" Evelyn asked.

"It's about 3:30, my dear," her mother replied.

Evelyn lay her head back upon the table, exhausted from the delivery. She turned to look at Richard and the baby.

"We have a son" she said. "We have a son."

Evelyn wasn't an only child, but she was seen and treated like a princess. Her debutante ball and coming out ceremony almost didn't happen because of the unexpected pregnancy. Coincidentally, her body supported the child in an almost invisible way for the first seven months. Mrs. Belle found a discreet seamstress who skillfully dressed Evelyn for the ball. Since it was her second trimester, Evelyn didn't have any bouts of sickness to contend with. Everything went off without a problem: she demonstrated her academic prowess and was presented, along with her future plans, for the entire entourage to witness at the ceremonial ball. Her accomplishments were well documented. Making the right connections through the Jack and Jill Society was an assumed next step in the process of securing her future.

"I was thinking we should make him a junior." Richard offered, referring to their son.

Richard had never expressed any input in the naming conversations that had taken place over the past three months. He'd left it all to his mother-in-law and young wife. He pretended to not have a strong opinion about what the name should be. But the truth was that he couldn't conceive of having a son and not giving him the family name *and* his first name. In the end, after much debate, they settled on a name.

Lawrence.

Their new son was Lawrence Anthony.

Apple Butter

Lawrence's list of favorite things was short. It wasn't because he was an insatiable young man. On the contrary, it was because he had found great satisfaction in his daily life and accomplishments over the years. As he began approaching the day when he would leave his parents' home to start bootcamp in the U.S. Army, he realized four things mattered to him: food, family, faith, and reputation. By the time he had reached the end of his first enlistment, he was proud of how diligently he had worked. Every day was a new day to be the best. He took no days off and perfected his physique. Lawrence liked his rigid way of living: forehead to the ground, focused on the mission at hand, love your people, and eat. He had grown into a young man who had very specific ideas about what success and successful black people should look like, act like, and how they should navigate life overall. Blame his parents for that. His father, the authoritarian who always led the family with strength, and his mother, who was the ultimate idyllic nurturer. She was the backbone of the household. Lawrence faithfully believed it was only a matter of time before he would be recognized for all the dedication and hard work he produced on base. He glanced down at the box in his hands that had just arrived from his mother and opened it to find one of his favorite things. Apple butter. Mason jarred. Quantity of three.

He recalled the anticipation of waiting in the kitchen for the long, slow cooking process. The caramelized sugar and apples heated up and then reduced into a smooth, deep brown, buttery sauce which reminded him of his next favorite thing: Vicki, his girlfriend. He'd nicknamed her apple butter. Her skin, the essence of her mind, and her eyes all reminded him of the dark, rich, deeply sweet taste of apple butter. In that order.

Making time to call Vicki, or to write her letters, was never a problem for Lawrence. He faithfully set aside time every week to call or drop an envelope in the mail for her. Today was a day for hearing the hypnotic sound of her voice. Lawrence glanced beyond the mail hall to take a look across the recreation room which was typically empty at that time of day. He didn't want anyone to overhear the way he speaks when he is on a call with her. Pure mush. His timing was impeccable with securing a place on the military base for their phone calls. He walked across the room and picked up the phone and dialed her number. He took a deep breath as the sound of the ringing reached his ears.

His station in New Jersey had a certain appeal to it and Lawrence had bought into its naval charm. Fort Monmouth military base was where he lived, but he could close his eyes and visualize the gorgeous Atlantic Ocean just five miles down the road. He dreamed of taking Vicki there, of kissing her on the boardwalk or taking her shopping. She would look smokin' hot in her yellow bikini contrasting against that smooth dark brown skin. Flawless from her head to her toenails. He knew from the moment he saw her that she was the one for him. His mother didn't care too much for her and he could never figure out why. He understood his mother's views and had ran through the mental checklist about Vicki before deciding to get serious. Vicki's background came with a certain pedigree that he affiliated with a great match. Similarly to him, she came from a family of black bourgeoisie activists, legacy and educated. He thought it was a win-win situation when he decided to make his interest in Vicki known to his parents. He was convinced she'd be everything his parents wanted for him. He couldn't recall the moment when he became completely absorbed by her. Maybe it was the first time he had been inside a jazz club and had heard such a sultry voice coming from the lips of a person. The mixture of the energy of the rhythm section and the saxophone, coupled with the energy that she exuded was an experience he didn't want to end. He couldn't keep his eyes off of her.

He quickly opened his eyes and returned his attention to the phone. He waited for the voice on the other end of the call. He set the box down.

"I said, have you called your parents yet?" Vicki asked.

"Not yet, you know I don't want to spend too much time talking about what I ought to be doing with my life."

"I know, but they worry about you and want to always know if they treat you bad in there."

"I can handle myself. Besides, I am an officer now. I made staff sergeant. I already told them I was serious about this army life. I plan to make this my career. Twenty years, baby. I can't wait to bring you down her to see the place. Man! You still got your yellow bikini I got you from Bamberger's?"

"Yes, baby," she cooed.

"Good. Make sure you keep it handy for the summertime. The blacks-only beach down here is so beautiful. It's going to be one of my best summers with you, the Atlantic, and these white folks all over me for my intelligence!"

"Why you have ta be so full of yourself?!" She laughed.

"I know you love it."

"I do." She sighed.

"So, how does it fit? Did I get the right size?" Lawrence asked.

"Oh. Yes, it's the right size. I just haven't tried it yet," Vicki replied dismissively.

"You do like it, right? I sent it more than two weeks ago. If it's not a good fit, I won't be upset, we can return it and get you what you like."

"Oh, no. I *love* it, Lawrence. I do. It just escaped my mind. Hey, when do you think they will pick you?"

"You mean assign me?"

"Whatever, yes, assign you."

"Assign me to what?"

"To a real job!"

Lawrence shifted his feet and switched off to lean his left shoulder onto the phone booth. He took a deep breath. To get the engineering position he wanted had been his greatest hurdle. So far, he had not met the qualifications, but he couldn't understand why or what was missing. The answers he received at all four of his requested post-application debriefs all felt ambiguous. He knew he was one of the hardest trained, focused and prepared soldiers there.

"Things don't work that easily over here for us."

"I just think it is ridiculous how much you make when you are one of the best soldiers they got!" she quipped.

"Yes, but that's not how it works. My pay is tied to my rank, and right now I am just moving up the ranks like everybody else. After a certain point, my merits will take me the rest of the way. Then you better watch out, baby! Get ready for me to take really good care of you, and it won't be with my parent's money either. So don't give it another thought. And please stop asking because you are starting to sound like my mother."

"Well, it's not easy waiting for you and your promises."

A powerful wave of emotion and muscle tension crossed Lawrence's chest, immediately followed by a heat rise to his cheeks. An unsettling sensation rose from his gut. He quickly switched his mind to the stacks of books waiting for him in his room. This feeling wasn't a new one. He felt it more often since leaving home and it felt like fear to him. He had decided long ago that it would never be coddled, only shut off with immediacy. He tracked his thoughts through the titles of each manual and book, then ran a mental count of how many, and with rapid succession, recalled a few facts from his study session the night before. Lastly, Lawrence brought his focus back to the awkward silence on the other end of the phone.

She spoke again, "You know I can't wait to see you for Christmas. Are you still approved to take some time, sweet love? Your old crew is planning to go up to Idlewild for a weekend. Jimmy's parents bought up some vacation property, so he is inviting us all to go up north to see the snow."

"Oooh weee! Jimmy loves show boatin,' don't he?! I bet you love it, huh?" Lawrence teased.

"You know what? I think now is the perfect time to call your mama 'cause I'm sure she loves it too! Bye!"

"Wait, ba—!"

There was a small giggle, a click, and then the dial tone. Lawrence clutched the receiver to his chest and leaned back against the phone booth with his eyes closed and his teeth exposed in the goofiest grin. He did a mental check of his heart and thought "yep, she's the one." Her ways were so exotic to him. He had never known a woman who could have him wrapped around her finger so tightly. Many of them had tried over the years, all throughout high school. He was often invited to be a debutante's escort to their coming out ball. That last year of high school had been crazy. Until Vicki, he had never even kissed a girl, but his mom and dad refused to believe him when they witnessed how girl after girl showed up to the house, crying, after they heard that he had enlisted in the Army. Lawrence had been glad his mom at least sided with him and signed the consent for him to voluntarily enlist at age seventeen. He had never seen his dad so angry, nor hold on to his anger for so long. As far as preachers go, he sure could hold a grudge. Years had passed and there was no change to his disposition. Right before turning to head back to Building 360 where the non-commissioned officers lived, Lawrence hung up the receiver and immediately picked it up again. He dialed the next number.

"Hello?" said Mrs. Anthony.

"Hi Mama".

Chiffon

Lawrence loved the sound of his mother's voice. It gave him such reassurance that although he had chosen an alternate path by deciding to not go to college right away and take over the family business, she still believed in him. When they sat at the dinner table night after night talking about the insurance company his grandfather had passed to them, and that it was now Lawrence's turn to take the helm, he had been honest about his feelings. It was not what he wanted for his life. If anyone would be upset, Lawrence felt like his mother should be the one. Everyone knew that it had originally been her father's insurance company. Instead, when heated moments that erupted between he and his father, she'd chosen to take a walk to the kitchen and bring back a single slice of chiffon cake she had reserved for Lawrence from the meetings she'd had with the ladies in her community organization. She did this just for Lawrence and he was convinced it was her attempt at breaking up the conversation a bit. As a result, chiffon cake came to be synonymous with calm for Lawrence. The light, fluffy, soft and springy cake with a hint of vanilla was delicately dusted with powdered sugar. It never overpowered him with sweetness. That is just how his mother's approach was with matters concerning him. Lawrence easily acquiesced to almost anything his mother asked of him.

"Hey Ma."

"L! Oh, my heavens! I knew it was you! How is it going and when are you going to get here!?"

Lawrence chuckled. He couldn't help but imagine her socialite superpowers began to ooze and spill right out onto the hardwood floors of their urban estate. He could picture her now with her perpetually perfect manicure, fourteen-inch pearl necklace, smooth chignon positioned neatly at the nape of her neck, kitten heels, and a sheath dress. Always elegant and ready with an answer for anyone. She believed in having conversations "seasoned with salt," like the Bible says. Mrs. Anthony was a frugal and sensible woman, disciplined and well-bred by grandmother and granddaddy Belle. Her warm, gingerbread-colored skin was silky smooth and her teeth pearly white. Whenever she laughed, she would throw her head back, and if you weren't laughing already, you involuntarily began to do so because hers was infectious. She was persuasive too. Anyone who lacked confidence in their purpose in life flocked like butterflies to nectar with Mrs. Anthony. By the time she was finished with them, they would walk out of the home with a goal and a plan to make it happen. All her qualities lent themselves well to her cause, her mission, and her passion. Activism. She didn't work outside the home, but, by golly, did she work inside! She didn't have time to cook elaborate meals, but she knew how to feed an army. And she did so every week as they hosted young men and women from the church while his father, the Reverend Anthony, facilitated the organization of the groups' plans for their participation in the Civil Rights Movement. Lawrence's parents' choice to move the family from Nashville, after the Reverend finished at Fisk University, was not coincidental. Mr. and Mrs. Anthony had a story almost identical to Lawrence's grandparents. The only difference was that they met at the end of their senior year in high school. After Lawrence's birth, they travelled all together up north during the great migration to Chicago with high school diplomas in hand. Once there, the family established their roots as activists, clergy and sole owners of a modest insurance agency. Mr. Anthony's induction into Sigma Pi Phi was seamless and occurred at a well-appointed time. He was following in the footsteps of his father-in-law by getting a college education too. Maintaining legacy. Afterwards, the Reverend moved the family again and took a teaching position back at Fisk, and once that was completed, the Anthony's found themselves once again at the forefront of the struggle for equality in the south. This time in Georgia. The Reverend was committed to the pursuit of excellence.

Lawrence's mother and the Reverend were a perfect complement for each other and reared Lawrence with consistent intent toward understanding his privilege and his plight. They wanted to be elbow deep in the movement while settling in a black community that was still able to prosper during these times in the south under Jim Crow law. Albany, Georgia had been perfect. They lived a life demonstrative of their message to self-segregate and not worry about the illusion of missed opportunities in other spaces. The message of self-segregating was the other reason Lawrence couldn't wait to get out of his parent's home. He vehemently disagreed with it, although he never said it out loud to their faces. He joined the Army to prove it. Lawrence had faith in the things he had been reading in the world history and U.S. history books, the Constitution, and the Bill of Rights. He poured over these documents regularly out of pure personal satisfaction. It was his honor and joy when he learned that you could be seventeen and join the military with parental consent.

"My dear, when will you be arriving?" his mother asked.

"Oh, ma, sorry. Right now, I am waiting on the approval, but I requested Saturday. Uh, by the twenty-first."

"That is perfect. Did you get the package I sent you?

"Yes, I have it right here. I can't believe you had the time to make this and mail it down to me, ma." Lawrence knew how busy her life became after he moved out. She concerned herself with educating and training others about voting, housing, money management, history, and the current events and news updates from other states across the country. She had a bit of a rebellious streak and if you didn't pay close enough attention, you could miss it because she hid it well. She skillfully tucked it behind her instructions and pushed it forward whenever time came to advocate for herself and others.

Lawrence glanced over at the box of apple butter jars and was filled with momentary courage.

"Hey ma, what is it about Vicki?"

He had never had this level of boldness with his mom before, but he had been thinking more and more about pursuing more than just a dating relationship with Vicki.

"She mentioned that she had spoken to you, and you were wanting to check up on me. Make sure everything was okay down here. Why haven't you mentioned her?"

"Well, Lawrence..." she began.

Lawrence was already dreading that he asked the question when she didn't refer to him as "L".

She heaved a heavy sigh and began again. "Lawrence. I am not going to spare my thoughts now that you have asked. I don't enjoy having these kinds of conversations. What we are building together in this community is a monumental task and very important for the future of this family. Hardships will be plentiful, and I believe that Vicki will add to your problems and not be the appropriate help mate that you deserve, baby."

Lawrence was stunned. Vicki had been right! All along he thought it was just her insecurities.

Mrs. Anthony continued, "Let me ask you a question Lawrence. How is it going over there? How are they treating you? How is the government treating you, my dear? Do I need to remind you of who you are? You are trying to do a noble thing because it is in the fabric of your upbringing, and I support you in finding your own way, but..."

"Ma, it is going great!" he interrupted. "I am in charge of a company of men, my skills are developing. Everything I have wanted to pursue, I can. They are treating me just fine." He lied.

Although it was true that he oversaw drills and practice and he was developing new skill sets, it really wasn't because he was openly welcomed. It was like his existence had to be rationed. Not too many of "those men" in and around all at once. None of the black soldiers would tell you they'd experienced anything different. Had his family been given a true glimpse into his daily life, they would see the segregation that existed within the confines of the base, complete with all the stressors and worries of an unfortunate confrontation. The combination of ambitious white men and ambitious black men all competing for the same jobs, and at the same time all pledging to serve the same country, was like oil and a flame. Together they could light up the world for the better. Left unattended, they could burn it down.

His mother paused a moment. "Vicki is too dark", she said bluntly. "I think you need to consider long and hard what you want your future children to have to endure walking around this nation with our background *and* with dark skin, L! It is asking for unnecessary trouble. It goes along much smoother when you have to deal with less differences. Please trust me on this one. There are plenty of beautiful young ladies who I am confident you will find a great deal in common with." Her voice was calm. "I am not asking you to be without someone, and I most definitely am not suggesting you date someone you don't love. I just know what I know about how the world works. Please don't go down that road."

Lawrence was stunned. He expected this kind of shit from his father. *There it is.* He finally uncovered why they had been able to stay together all these years. They weren't as different as he had perceived. They were two peas in a pod. Did they both see him as a black stain on their progress? As if she could read his thoughts, Mrs. Anthony interrupted the silence.

"You know, your father is sitting here," she said.

"Go ahead and pass the phone." Lawrence said flatly.

There was silence for a few moments, along with some mumbled words in the background. Lawrence could tell his father was giving his mother a hard time about getting on the phone.

Fatigues

Lawrence shifted his weight and leaned on the phone booth. He changed his mind, and using his foot, hooked a nearby chair and pulled it close enough to sit down while he waited for his father's voice to acknowledge him. Lawrence glanced down at his uniform. If there was one thing that made him uncomfortable about being in the Army, it was the field uniform. It was used daily for fieldwork and intended for combat duty. The green camouflage was a necessary garment, protective, and easy to keep clean. It was a blend of fabrics, some cotton and some synthetic fibers. He could feel the difference on his skin, and it made him uncomfortable. It reminded him of his father. The Reverend Richard Anthony had lucked out when he knocked up young Ms. Belle out of wedlock all those years ago. Richard had the look, but he didn't have the pedigree. All of that came to him like a gift, a dowry almost, when he married Evelyn. The Belle's had taken Richard under their wing and taught him everything they wanted him to be for their daughter's sake. However, something always felt off about it all. Like a cotton and synthetic blended battle uniform. Real and fake. Weak and strong. Lawrence never heard any of the other soldiers complain about the comfort of the fatigues, but for him, depending on the weather conditions he encountered, he could find himself not protected as well as he could have been. And just like camouflage, the good Reverend knew how to hide himself among enemies. Yep, they reminded him of his father.

Lawrence continued to wait on the phone.

"Hello?" his father finally said.

"Hey, sir, how is everything?"

"Well, you know, things are still tense around here ever since the election last week. You should have been here. Helping instead of running away."

Well, that didn't take long, Lawrence thought.

"Sir, I don't understand why the insistence that I cannot also make a difference from right here inside the military? Our country needs more men who are able to lead, have courage, and are willing to go where the needs are for securing our freedom here at home. You are on one side of the battle, and I am on the other side, sir. With all due respect. The way I see it, it is a two-pronged approach." Lawrence finished and waited. He had become significantly more emboldened with the manner in which he spoke to his dad over the past three years but definitely a more forceful approach by phone than if they were face to face.

His father continued as if he hadn't heard anything Lawrence had said. "The movement is strengthening, and my only son is wasting his life by voluntarily running to defend a country that won't defend him. Right here at home."

Lawrence had enough. He couldn't bear to hold it in any longer. "Is that what you think? Sir? Do you recall the time we drove to visit grandmother and granddaddy over in Alabama? Well, that was the time I lost all respect for you. So, we are on the same page."

"I see," his father said.

Lawrence could sense his father recoil through the phone at the sound of his comment. This only gave Lawrence more courage to continue. "You always raised me to be proud of who we are, our family, our heritage, and the work of our hands. Remember you always said, 'we have money, we have our reputation, there is no reason to hide.' Do you remember?" Lawrence tried to get his mouth to stop moving before he took it too far, but there was no turning back. "Tell me why, sir, why then that no sooner we made it to that Alabama diner off Route 72 did you hide away who you are? Who we are!"

Lawrence could feel the indignation and heat rise from his belly as he recalled the day. The drive from Tennessee had been long and Lawrence was hungry, so his father pulled into the diner and walked in to order food. He had asked Lawrence to remain in the car. After it seemed to take too long, Lawrence got out and entered the front door of the diner to find his father sitting at the lunch counter.

"What do you want, boy? And who told you that you could use that front door?" His father demanded from his perch on the stool. Lawrence was completely confused until the flood of all the conversations he had overhead in the living room of his family home came crashing down in an instant. His father was high yellow and could easily pass for white. Lawrence, however, had his mother's gingerbread complexion and looked like a stain walking through that swinging door that afternoon in the diner.

"I said, what do you want, boy?! You better go back where you came from." His father spoke once more and then turned on the stool to face the waitress again. Something about his father's demeanor frightened him so Lawrence immediately went back to the car without saying a word. By the time his father returned to the car, Lawrence had cried himself to sleep. He had never been so angry as he'd been that day. Here his dad was *passing* and sitting among the white townsfolk and addressing his only son like he was a non-entity or dreg of society. How could he betray the family and his work in the community like this? Lawrence had since wondered if his mother knew that his father had another persona when traveling through the south. As of that moment, he could see them both clearly for who they really were.

"You whine and complain too much, son. We needed a meal that day. Like every day. In life you will learn that your mother and I protected you too much and that you will need to step up and sometimes do things you need to survive. Otherwise, I expect when you have a family of your own you will have your wife make all the hard decisions."

Once again, Lawrence was suspended in disbelief at the things that could come out of his father's mouth. The conversation ended on that note. He replaced the receiver and leaned back in the chair. He took deep breaths and allowed the building tightness across his chest to subside. He took a few extra moments to run through his mental exercises of counting objects, recalling items and circling back to the space he was in.

Screw them.

Monday

The "smell of dawn rising" was how Lawrence liked to think of his mornings on base. He could distinguish the scent of salt water in the air as he took the last lap of his pre-dawn, six-mile run. Today, the air was cold and crisp at Fort Monmouth. With his miles complete, he took his time getting showered and dressed. If there was anything he brought with him to the military, it would be his attention to detail and his sharp way of dressing. Every part of his standard issue uniform was intact. He was like his mother in this way: never a pin out of place. This commitment to excellence began to easily trickle over into his life as the Parts Personnel on the base. He had rotated through multiple work assignments over the years. First physical training instructor, tent pitching, camp sanitation, then repairing and extending roads. No matter where he was assigned, he worked his ass off. Or, as they said at home, "as if working for the Lord." Similarly, as his peers teased, "like ol' John Henry." Either way, Lawrence was known to start a task and then relentlessly hammer away at it with all his might, with his will power going beyond his own physical limitations. Right now, his personal focus was to get assigned to cryptography. Lawrence was ready to specialize, and he already had his hands on the instruction manuals. He studied for hours every night to ensure he'd be ready when the opportunity presented itself. Just as he was headed out the door, he spotted another parts employee from his team, Chad. He knew each of his team mates well. He had a conviction that if you were going to potentially go to battle with someone, it is necessary to know them as well as you can. Chad immediately saluted.

"At ease," Lawrence directed.

"Hey, did you hear? We have the largest units of enlisted because of voluntary sign ups. More than drafted ones," Chad said, his tone proud.

"That's right. Men do what they need to do for this country. If we want change, we got to be willing to work for it. Are you a draftee or volunteer?" Lawrence inquired.

"I volunteered, man."

Lawrence laughed. "I know, I just have to check periodically to see if your story changes. So, why does it sound like there is more you gotta say?"

"Well, rumor has it that some transfers may start happening. And those transfers might be over to Fort Bragg."

"Is that so?"

"Oh yeah."

"Oh yeah?"

"You know what's waiting for us over there at Bragg don't cha?" Chad asked. "They have all the special ops. They are the 911 for the President himself!"

"Hell yes!" Lawrence said. "Thanks, man. I can feel it. My shot is coming."

As Chad and Lawrence made their way down to the facilities building, they recognized the rest of the crew bounding up the stairs toward the front door to get started for the day.

Lawrence had just made it inside the building when the men began standing at attention.

With a quick glance he saw why.

"Good Morning, sir!" Lawrence immediately saluted and stood in line with the other men before Major General Campau. His heart rate remained steady, but his mind was running a mile a minute. It was a curious situation to see the Major General so early in their part of the base.

"At ease, gentlemen," the Major General responded.

"Sir, to what do we owe the pleasure, sir?" Lawrence said, as staff sergeant of the crew.

"I am here to ask that you please send over this list of men from your unit for a meeting with me. I want to personally see to it that you also attend."

"Yes, sir. Absolutely, sir," Lawrence replied.

Just as quickly as he had arrived, the Major General was gone again, and the entire unit let out spontaneous yelps and whoops. A great majority of the unit had no desire to make the military their career, but for the others, this was a fast-track opportunity and they knew it.

Lawrence opened the folder to read the names of the men who made the list.

Chad Johnson

Robert Smith

Ronald Robinson

Daniel Jones

Leon Booker

Lawrence Anthony

A.J. Stickney

The men clamored together and huddled up to discuss the turn of events.

"Do you think the white boys got their list hand delivered by the Major General?" joked A.J.

A.J. was older than the rest of the men by three years. He was from a family with a sharecropping history. A.J. made it blatant that he was in the military for the income and medical benefits. However, this latest offer to transfer to Bragg clearly had him caught up with everyone else's excitement.

"Hell naw!" shouted Chad. Everyone was laughing while Leon broke out a stash whiskey. They took turns taking a swig from the bottle. When it got to Lawrence's turn, he declined. Always setting the example.

"Those cats at Bragg are gonna see how to really get a job done!"

At the appointed time that day, Lawrence arrived at Major General Campau's office with the six fellow soldiers. They were a mix of non-commissioned officers and enlisted crew. As he glanced around the room, he grew acutely aware of the excellence among him. These fellow crewmen were the best of the best in the black unit. Dare he say, also among the best of across base. As the meeting progressed, all of the details were revealed to the men standing there. This was the opportunity that Lawrence had been waiting on. A transfer. There would be an intelligence team. Red Dog for the President. The process would involve medical reviews beginning later that day and then a transfer, at a time later to be determined, to Fort Bragg in North Carolina. Fort Bragg was the location Lawrence and his unit talked about like a fantasy.

This was his lucky shot at shifting his future so that he could finally follow through with his plan to return home a fully independent man. There would be no way his father could deny the impact he would begin to have in life and for the country. His mother would see that all the dark skinned-light skinned mumbo jumbo was piss in the wind.

The men were dismissed to immediately report to the hospital located in Building 209, Allison hall. They all arrived at the appointed time and lined up to check in. Every year they receive a standard routine physical fitness and medical examination processes, but this time, they also underwent extensive psychological testing which Lawrence and the others had never experienced at that level before.

One by one, the men completed their rounds of tests and interviews with the medical staff. The nurse on duty passed out the paperwork: waivers and the like for everyone to sign.

At the end of the day, they were all given a cocktail injection. The super soldier mix. This, as explained, was the infusion they all would need to be able to experience a heightened ability to undergo more intense trials, increased thinking, and speed and endurance, among other things. They all signed the release.

Later that morning, as Lawrence snuggled up to his cryptography manuals, he studied with a new fervor. *Hell yes,* he thought. *Hell yes.* After an hour a familiar feeling began to consume his belly, chest and throat. He closed the manuals, leaned over the bedside, and placed them on the floor as he took slow deep breaths and fought back the tears forming under the closed lids of his eyes. Upon opening them, he glanced around the room, taking notice of the photos he had on display. All of them strategically placed for whenever he needed reminding that to be the best, you must always be *the best of the best.* Lawrence took his time to focus on the images of his family, Vicki and the neighborhood back home. Thinking about what it takes to make it big and become a success was a constant developing theme for him. No one could really understand what it takes for him to stay on the grind the way he does. As his eyes rested on the last photo of him and Vicki, he took another slow, deep breath and silently prayed a word of thanks for the events in the earlier part of the day with the medical staff. Lawrence was not a praying man, but when faced with the possibility of losing his emotional shit in front of anyone on base, he couldn't find a better time than that moment to begin a new habit. It was a mortifying thought, beyond imagination, that he might possibly be in over his head with the new job offer. The promises of what the medical injections could do for his physical exertion was a welcomed bonus to the offer awaiting him and his crew at Fort Bragg. His biggest hope was that the medicine would eliminate the headaches and weakness that had been happening more frequently. As his thoughts lingered on that possibility, he became hopeful again and got up from the bed, switched into his physical training gear and prepared himself to take his second run of the day. *I ain't got time for laying around.*

Lawrence bounded out the door and down the steps into a warm-up jog. The faint sound of his shoes on the pavement, the cadence of his own footsteps, and the sound of his heartbeat in his ears was like a symphony and a soundtrack for the moment. He welcomed the wind on his face as it comingled with the perspiration that began to form as he ran faster. The coolness he felt on those runs were always the perfect counter sensation he needed for offsetting the fatigue, stress and anger he secretly endured most days. Long before joining the Army, Lawrence discovered the impact that running had on him. From a time as early as his freshman year in high school, he could recall the insular moments of overwhelm and overstimulation by the sounds, smells and sights around him in class, riding in the car with friends, or in the pew in the back of the church. He couldn't recall why he began going on jogs, but the calm and clarity that he experienced afterwards was therapeutic.

He rounded the corner on his way back to his building even though he didn't feel quite ready to end his run. It was time to get ready for work. The mundanity of life working in the parts warehouse was predictable at best. Try as he might, Lawrence could not convince himself that this job was given to him for any other reason except to fulfill a duty that no one else really wanted. Slowly, he prepared his shave kit and uniform, showered and meticulously dressed himself for the day. Lawrence arrived on time at the warehouse, clocked in and grabbed the stack of papers from the inbox tray that rested on the counter. Sitting on top of the pile was a large parts request that he didn't recognize. He checked the issuing officer signature and compared it to the approval list hanging on the wall on a clipboard to his right.

Joshua Fitzsimmons.

Lawrence immediately went to the issuing officer, his equal in rank, to inquire about the lateness of the request as it was attached to an *urgent please* addendum. This wasn't the first time Fitzsimmons had submitted last minute requests like this. Lawrence hated nothing more than being ill prepared or circumventing rules and processes and Fitzsimmons seemed to embody both on a regular basis. The encounter ended in an argument, and it wasn't the only one of the day. Lawrence was reminded of the potential power of mixing oil and flames. A metaphor his mother used when describing potential arguments with white people. She would say "oil is good for cooking and so are flames, but when you mix them together, you better know what you are doing." By the time Lawrence made it to the mess hall for supper that night, he was exhausted.

That evening, for the first time, he thought he heard a voice in his head. But what was it saying? He pushed the thoughts aside as he crossed over to the next building, turned the corner, and sprinted up the stairs to his building. There was a letter on his bed. He had submitted a request to have a civilian visitor. Vicki. He opened the letter and was overwhelmed with joy. It was an approval. This was shaping up to be the best day ever. Even with the troubles at work.

His feelings of ill health began to shift as he grabbed his water and quickly walked over to the medical building to discuss and review the side effects of the new vitamin mix they were being injected with. After asking around his unit, none of the other men had reported feeling any different, so he didn't let on that he was feeling anything either. As soon as he had an opportunity, he called Vicki to tell her about the approval and that she could drive over for a visit.

After his second medical review was completed, he waited for the lab reports to return. The next hour, he received an all clear and decided it was all in his head. Maybe he was just exhausted from the extra work, extra stress, the excitement of his pending transfer and a visit from apple butter.

The following morning, the secretary issued the orders from Major General Campau. Lawrence's transfer was approved, and he was to report to Fort Bragg in a week. He imagined himself pulling up to Fort Bragg, the gates flanked by armed MPS. He would hand them a copy of the orders and then roll right in.

This was his dream come true.

Hell yes. Any time, Anyhow, Anywhere.

Tuesday

Lawrence and the rest of the men received their instructions to arrive at building #250 in order to be briefed prior to transferring. They were to meet with the receiving team for a few hours before heading back for rifle practice and training. Lawrence crossed the threshold of the entrance and on his left, he could see his file was ready, in the office, on top of the desk. He walked across the room, took a seat next to Chad and waited. After a time that seemed like an eternity, the commanding officer walked into the room and over to the desk. Lawrence's file was pulled from the top of the stack, opened, the pages were flipped through and placed back on the desk. The commanding officer made a grunting sound and looked up. It was hard to discern if the sound was one of approval, dismay or surprise. He gave the standard welcome to everyone and instructed each soldier to see the secretary on his way out to receive the details for a bunk assignment.

Lawrence stood up and began making his way to the space where the secretary stood. As he passed by, the commanding officer spoke up.

"Welcome to the team Anthony", calling Lawrence by his last name. "This is a special opportunity for folks like you. I hope you are not taking it lightly".

This bristled Lawrence's pride, dignity and heart. He couldn't contain himself from blurting out a *clarifying* question.

"Sir, folks like me? How?"

Without hesitation the commander stood up and said, "Blacks. For blacks, Anthony. I know you boys are mostly just looking for a warm meal, a paycheck and some medical, but listen to me about this assignment", he paused and carefully glanced around at the other men in the room and returned his gaze back to Lawrence. "You better not screw this up. This is a special opportunity for folks like you."

Lawrence chose to remain quiet. He accepted the answer. It was honest. He decided to acknowledge it as blunt exposure to the real thoughts and perspectives of the man he would be perhaps serving under. Lawrence knew that he would rather be aware of the truth in a man's heart, than to be blind sighted later in an unfortunate conflict. He knew how to handle people better this way.

The highly anticipated meeting continued without much fanfare and the collection of men were attentive to all details and instructions for the timing of departure and for the assignment of duties. After 40 minutes they were issued their official orders and dismissed.

As soon as he was released from the meeting, Lawrence found a pay phone to call Vicki. There was no answer, so he called his mother.

"Ma, I didn't get the release I expected, and I am sorry I didn't call you before now". He knew he was lying because he never submitted a request for himself, he only wanted the approval for Vicki's visit.

"It's okay honey, we would have begun to get worried if we didn't hear anything by tomorrow. We know you. Always focused. Please keep us posted on when we can see you again".

"Ok, ma".

Excitedly, he hung up the phone and tried Vicki one more time.

No answer.

He hung up the receiver slowly and took it as a good sign that she wasn't answering the phone.

She is on her way.

Lawrence's thoughts were interrupted by the sound of a nearby closing door. He glanced down at his watch and realized it was almost time for practice. Rifle practice was one of his favorite training requirements but lately Lawrence worried that some indifference might've been creeping in as he was waiting for the opportunity to do a job that he liked beyond the basics.

For now, it doesn't matter, he thought, *I have new orders anyway.*

He started walking to practice and quickened his pace as he caught a visual of the men lining up to collect a weapon from the facility. Lawrence unlocked the door and began the checkout process as his mind drifted back to Vicki, wondering if she had remembered to leave on time. They were training for more than an hour when Lawrence decided to step away.

"Hey, Fitzimmons! Take over."

Lawrence tossed to him the facility keys and made his way back to his quarters. He was ready to get out of there so that he could prepare himself before Vicki's arrival.

***

Lawrence took his time taking a shower. The water was tepid and refreshing to his skin after the time spent outside in practice. He took a glance into the small wall mirror while he slowly applied some shaving cream across the stubble beginning to show along his jawline. As the water stuttered, intensified in pressure, and became warmer, he allowed his eyes to close and for his shoulders to relax. He took a few deep breaths, slowly inhaling and exhaling. The moment he'd rehearsed all day in his mind drifted back into his thoughts. The anticipation of Vicki's visit was almost more than he could bear as he attempted to complete any daily routine or work that morning. This was the weekend he had been waiting for and her bus would be arriving shortly after 1 o'clock. There were no plans in place except to tell her three things: how much he loved her, acknowledge the rift that existed between her and his family, and to share the good news about his reassignment. He opened his eyes and finished shaving, rinsed well and stepped out of the shower. The heat of the midday was already causing the bunkhouse to fill with a humid warmth. He grabbed a towel and his toiletry kit. Any other day he would have skipped primping and preening, but it was no time for showing up with dry and ashy skin. Lawrence clipped and shaped his nails, taking extra care to smooth out the edges, and to moisturize his skin with the cocoa butter he kept in his bag. Along the bottom he uncovered his bottle of *Pour Monsieur* cologne, which he only wore on special occasions. He used it sparingly since he didn't know when he would be able to pluck down the dollars for more now that he is footing his own bills. He finished fastening the last buttons, laced his boots, and took a look in the mirror for a last, proud, glance at his rank patches. Lawrence grabbed his car keys and turned to leave when Chad walked in.

"Sir?"

"Yes?"

"The office was closed, sir." He said, panicked.

"At ease. What do you mean?" Lawrence asked.

"The storage spot. For the rifles. It's closed, sir. I can't find nobody with an extra key."

"Find Fitzsimmons, he has my key."

"Fitz is gone sir. He had plans off base tonight."

"Ok, but what's the problem? Why do you need to get back in there?"

There was a long pause while Lawrence waited for a response.

"I still have mine, sir. Mine and A.J.'s."

Lawrence stood there for a moment feeling sick. This was the worst moment to have something as important as guns and Vicki clash and compete for his time. His impatience quickened.

"Very well, I will sign off. Give them to me."

Chad stepped outside the door and immediately brought back the rifles and handed them over to Lawrence. They didn't have access to the standard pink sheets for signing and logging the rifles as returned, so Lawrence pulled out an old notebook from across the room and scrawled out a receipt and a note. He signed the bottom.

"Anybody ask, you just tell them that I got 'em," Lawrence said.

Chad took the slip of paper and turned and left. Lawrence stood there for a moment deciding on what to do next. He couldn't leave them unsecured in the bunkhouse.

Dammit, he thought.

As he stepped out into the bright sunlight, he could hear the engines of faraway vehicles, and the relaxed murmurs of conversations being conducted across the field from where he stood. His anxious eye gaze tracked the open expanse that lay in front of him. The grassy areas had taken on the brown and dry look of long hours in the sun with an occasional patch of bare soil that was easily demarked as a soft path worn from walking back and forth to the parking station.

Lawrence took this path and quickened his steps while allowing his mind to slowly accept the choice he was making by keeping the guns with him. Lawrence was not in the habit of doing things out of order or against protocol, as a result, the unnerving feelings that welled up threatened to overcome his usual demeanor. Whenever faced with difficult decisions, Lawrence had never faltered. Finally reaching his car, he popped open the trunk and carefully placed them inside and double checked the safety lock. He exhaled so sharply that the crescendo of the trunk locking was overpowered by the sound his body expressed. By the time he had clicked on his seat belt and cranked up the car, all of his anxieties about breaking the rules had dispersed and the only thing on his mind was the 8 minute drive to the rail and bus station to get Apple Butter.

Lawrence he couldn't help but think about the parts of himself she doesn't yet know about him. The parts that are unsavory. The spaces he saw as darkened and necessary parts of himself that are up at night, all night, pouring over books, charts, programs and operating manuals just to get it right and become the best. The inner drive toward becoming perfect in his knowledge. The relentless perseveration on what it means to be a man, a provider, protector, and a lover. The inner most parts of him that cannot dial down at night so that he may rest, until he reaches a level of success that will warrant his existence. He is met with a deep resistance in his heart and his mind. He cannot allow her to see him this way. Marriage is out of the question, and he just can't imagine not telling her the truth while face to face. He owes her that much.

She just won't agree, and he knows it.

This last realization drifts slowly to the back of his mind as he takes his foot off the gas to coast the car into the pick-up zone of the station. It feels like an eternity before he sees her emerge from the doorway. He quickly releases the lock, throws the car into park position, and jumps out to jog around to sweep her up into his arms. The soft bulge of her belly against the firmness of his is compressed with the pressure of their embrace, while the vibration of their collective laughter travels along their merged bodies. She plants dozens of small kisses

all along his neck, jawline and cheeks in rapid fire succession. Finally giving her one last squeeze, Lawrence slowly lowers her to her feet. After locking into her eye gaze, he finds the

reassurance he needs to plant a long and sweet kiss on her lips. He closes his eyes to inhale

deeply. They stand there in silence for several moments until Vicki finally spoke up.

"Baby, are you okay?"

Lawrence didn't expect her to be so bold or to notice this quickly. He wondered if the time apart had made her more sensitive to the shifts in his emotions or thoughts, or that perhaps he had become less skilled at hiding them.

"Yes. I'm cool baby." Lawrence said easily.

He reached down to grab her bag and noticed there wasn't one except for what was on her shoulder. He stretched out his hand to lift the strap and relieve her from the weight of it when she took a step back, crossed her arms and leaned back onto her left foot. Lawrence couldn't think fast enough to come up with an answer more appropriate than the one he'd given. He used to be able to easily finesse her with a joke or funny comeback, but his mind seemed to have a lock on it.

"Really, baby, I'm fine. More than fine, I have great news about my next assignment."

Lawrence offered.

"Why do you do that?" Vicki demanded.

"Do what?"

"You keep pushing me away. Why do you do that? I want to be closer to you." Vicki softly spoke.

Lawrence hadn't planned to get into this conversation so quickly after picking her up from the station. He had planned for them to have dinner, dance a little, do a whole lotta huggin' and kissin', and *then* bring up the real-life stuff.

"Lawrence? Are you listening to me?" Vicki's voice faltered a little.

"Do you think I am a robot Vicki? Do you think I don't have feelings? What happens if I leave here and I haven't accomplished what I need to have accomplished? What happens if I take a look back and this wasn't the right choice?

"Do you mean us?" She asked. "Are you saying that maybe we aren't your 'right choice'? "I am talking about the military baby. This army thing. The answer is this; If I haven't

made the right choice, then I have to start all over. Do you get that? Some women just wait around to find a good man to marry, and they think afterwards that you get to live happily ever after. Well, it doesn't happen. The way I see it, a man has to show up day in and day out. Day after day after day, Vicki. We don't get days off. I am busting my tail over here on this base and do you think I get the justice I deserve? There is no space to complain about it. Me and my men are under a certain kind of pressure and I know that I will make my own way eventually. Until then, I don't have time to go down deep and express my feelings. When you love a man with scars, you love a troubled man. You are loving a toxic man. You wouldn't be able to handle it."

"Lawrence, I just want you to trust me enough to fall into me or lean into me when you need it. I don't have all the answers. All I know is that I will be honest with you and I want to be the one who reminds you of who you are outside of that uniform, your family and your ambitions. You are not the money you make. If the day ever comes when I see you as just a way to get a cute house and some kids, then that is the day I am no longer truly loving you. Lawrence, I need you to meet me inside *that* heart space. Show up with your whole self. That is what I want. That is all I am asking for."

He stood there for a moment thinking about the words he heard coming from her mouth. Everything she said made sense to him and he wanted to reciprocate it. He wanted to receive it. Lawrence fell into another round of silence as he thought about getting off the sidewalk of the station and getting on with the evening. The original plan for dinner had to shift and now the new plan was to return the guns before driving her to a hotel until he could figure out family visitor housing. He grabbed her hand in silence, opened the door to the passenger side and waited for her to step in. Despite the conversation so far, Lawrence was still far more excited in anticipation of the time they would be able to have together. The approval was only for 24 hours and he didn't want to spend it all in discourse that would leave them both worked up and stressed out. He closed her door and moved confidently back to the driver's side and quickly got them back on the road heading towards the base. The conversation had moved into a softer zone of catch-up on the neighborhood gossip as they pulled into drive of the compound. Lawrence noticed the gathering of MPs seemed to be excessive around the entrance, he made a mental note of it, regarded it as a possible time for shift change and slowly pulled up to a lesser manned booth. He rolled his window down and lifted his credentials out of his back pocket, put the car into park and turned to greet the booth soldier. Lawrence's eyes were met with the barrel of a gun, he heard a gunshot, Vicki's scream and then darkness. When he awoke in the stockade, he searched his body for injuries and found none. He was asked to remove his rank patches.

Lawrence couldn't stop the tears from flowing.

Dishonorable

Lawrence's whole body feels like a dead weight and every blink of his eyes arrives in slow motion. He awakens with the vivid memory of his desire to die and the weight of hopelessness. He felt trapped and out of control of his own life when he decided to end it all instead of removing his patches and accept a demotion in rank. He had met with the assigned JAG officer and learned of the charges against him. Everything that happened at the entrance to the base 6 months ago was recorded in the court documents that had been reviewed with him over the course of time while working with the army psychiatrist. Vicki was dead and he was being dishonorably discharged. He lay there fully dressed, numb and unable to distinguish if the feelings were medication induced or if he had finally given up his spirit. Lawrence glanced down to his wrists where his scars had healed as softened lines all along the circumference. A heaviness settled more deeply on his chest as he thought back to the day it all happened. He closed his eyes again and didn't open them again until he could push the thoughts away to focus on something new. He awaited the last knock on the door to deliver his release documents so he could head home. The guilt of being the cause for Vicki getting shot that day by an MP was more than he could stomach. The details were still unclear, but the documents he'd read detailed the series of events. The MPs knew that the car was holding the missing firearms,

Vicki hadn't been identified as registered yet for the visit and Lawrence had been classed as AWOL. The myriad of mishaps was the perfect storm for the confrontation that happened when Lawrence pulled into the entrance that day. Mid thought, Lawrence heard a knock on the stockade door and immediately sat up on the bed where he lay. Major General Campau entered into the room. Lawrence began to stand up and salute, but was immediately deterred.

"As you were." Campau ordered.

Lawrence sat back onto the bunk. He was stunned and silent with the unexpected visit.

"I understand you got yourself into a whole mess. I spent quite a bit of my personal time trying to figure this out soldier. I hand-picked you for Red Dog then you go and pull this shit."

Lawrence could feel the numbness fall away and his pride rise up inside his chest. After all the commitment and dedicated work he had put into his first and second enlistments, he knew for sure that Red Dog assignment wasn't some bone to be thrown at him in an act of philanthropy. Hell no. He had earned that spot. Lawrence remained silent, yet, increasing in resolve.

"I reviewed your file myself Private Anthony...Lawrence."

Campau took a seat and removed his cap. Lawrence was stunned at the sound of his first name coming out of the major's mouth and could feel the fog lift from his brain a bit more as his alertness increased.

"I reviewed it myself because I knew first-hand the commitment and dedication you have put into your time here. It's why I chose your team. So, I finally took a visit and had a talk with the Board on your behalf. You'll get an honorable discharge son. You earned that. You need to get home to that baby of yours and see what you can still make out of life for yourself."

Lawrence was stunned with the news of a baby. *Vicki had been pregnant?*

"The weapons charges and AWOL are all dropped. I asked to be the one to inform you that your pregnant girlfriend was able to deliver a baby before her untimely passing and after living with surrogates, the baby was picked up by your mother and taken back home."

Lawrence's face softens and tears involuntarily begin to fall from his eyes as they turn into a cooled cast iron shade of black.

Campau stands up to replace the cap on his head and Lawrence stands too. Campau reaches his hand out the door and pulls in the discharge documents for Lawrence. He places them into his hands and steps aside from the doorway leaving space for Lawrence to exit.

Lawrence takes the forms with a long pause when he catches a glimpse of himself in the mirror across the room.

"I have my name. And I have my honor," he said out loud.

Lawrence saluted himself. He saluted his future.

The Year: 2020

Reading my dad's name in print sent a chill up my right arm. Lawrence. I allowed my gaze and mind to drift away from the military documents in my hands that I'd been reading and slowly took a sip of my coffee. I glanced back to the clock, the hoard of books and the CDs surrounding me as I tried to control the flood of questions that were crashing down. The reports that detailed my father's first attempt at suicide during his enlistment is my favorite one. I know that *sounds* crazy, but it chronicled one of the first memories he had ever shared with me of his time in the Army. It seemed like such a harrowing tale. Screw that, let me be honest with you; I thought he was lying. Perhaps, at best, he was exaggerating what really happened that day when he couldn't remember why he was in the stockade removing his rank patches. Maybe that is why this part of his life intrigues me so. Why it is my favorite. I think it is the way I can visualize his strength and vitality in those moments on his army base, juxtaposed against my firsthand knowledge of the man I had grown up with. An overt flirt, woman loving, erratic, brilliant, humorous, scary, lean and wiry, bible quoting, cocky son-of-a-gun. Inside me grew a deep admiration as well as hatred for all I knew my dad to be. Decades ago, sometime around my fifteenth birthday, I'd begun to follow the breadcrumbs that would take me on endless journeys with books trying to understand and label what was wrong with my dad. But today I hit the motherload while standing in his apartment waiting for the 1-800-hoard team to arrive to haul away the mess. This last set of binders jammed in a corner (and covered in lord knows what) gave me all my answers. Another chill rushed over me. This time it ran through my body, and I could feel my underarms and the space under my breasts begin to pool with clammy sweat. I felt a sickening feeling well up and involuntary tears began to form. He didn't make any of it up. All the stories he told, history he shared, and every bombastic tale of accomplishments, obstacles, mental health challenges, and intentional adversaries were true. Damn.

My name is Alexis Anthony.

Daddy, I salute you.

ABOUT THE AUTHOR

After noticing the intense love her daughter had for listening to stories from her childhood, Maya decided to reflect on stories that revealed more about her dad who'd shared about his life as a black man in the military during the Jim Crow era. Maya Bechi, the mother of two, is an educator of high school students with neuro differences and an advocate for mental health and mental hygiene.

Robson and Puritan publishes books from a niche market of Indie Authors that reflect living a lifestyle unmatched and untethered while sometimes being underestimated.

We welcome your comments and suggestions for the content.
Write to us at robsonandpuritan@gmail.com
Robson and Puritan, LLC • P.O. Box 1107 • Cypress, TX 77410